To: ....

From: ....

First published in paperback in Great Britain by HarperCollins Children's Books in 2009

1 3 5 7 9 10 8 6 4 2

ISBN-13: 978-0-00-730374-8

HarperCollins Children's Books is a division of HarperCollins Publishers Ltd.

77-85 Fulham Palace Road, Hammersmith, London W6 8JB.

Visit our website at: www.harpercollins.co.uk

Printed and bound in China

If I Were the Easter Bunny

Illustrated by Louise Gardner

HarperCollins *Children's Books*

If I were the Easter Bunny,
I'd wake my friends up early.

If I were the Easter Bunny, I'd fill my Easter basket with lots of chocolate eggs...

...and hide them all over the meadow
for everyone to find.

If I were the Easter Bunny,
we'd have a happy hopping competition...

...and an Easter-egg-and-spoon race.
Ready, steady ... go!

If I were the Easter Bunny,
we'd make pretty Easter bonnets...

...and I'd lead the way in the Easter parade.
Quick, march!

If I were the Easter Bunny,
I'd have a yummy picnic tea...

...and at the end of the day, everyone would
go home with a bag of tasty treats.

But, best of all, if I were the Easter Bunny,
I'd save the very last egg, just for...